Baby Animals

S0-FQM-648

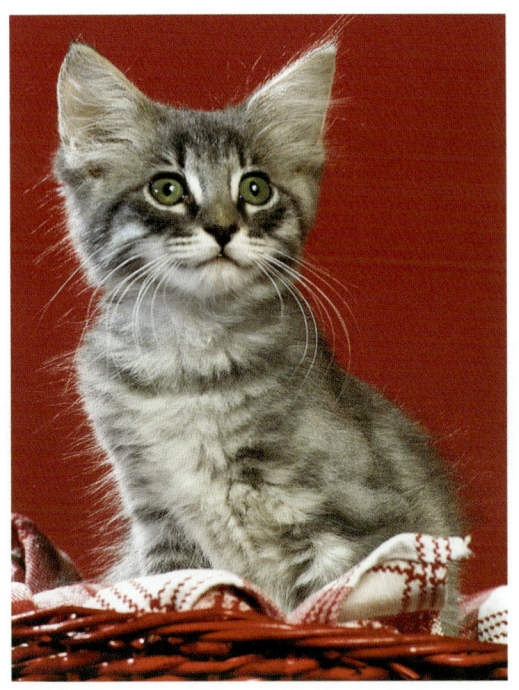

written by Pam Holden

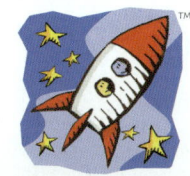

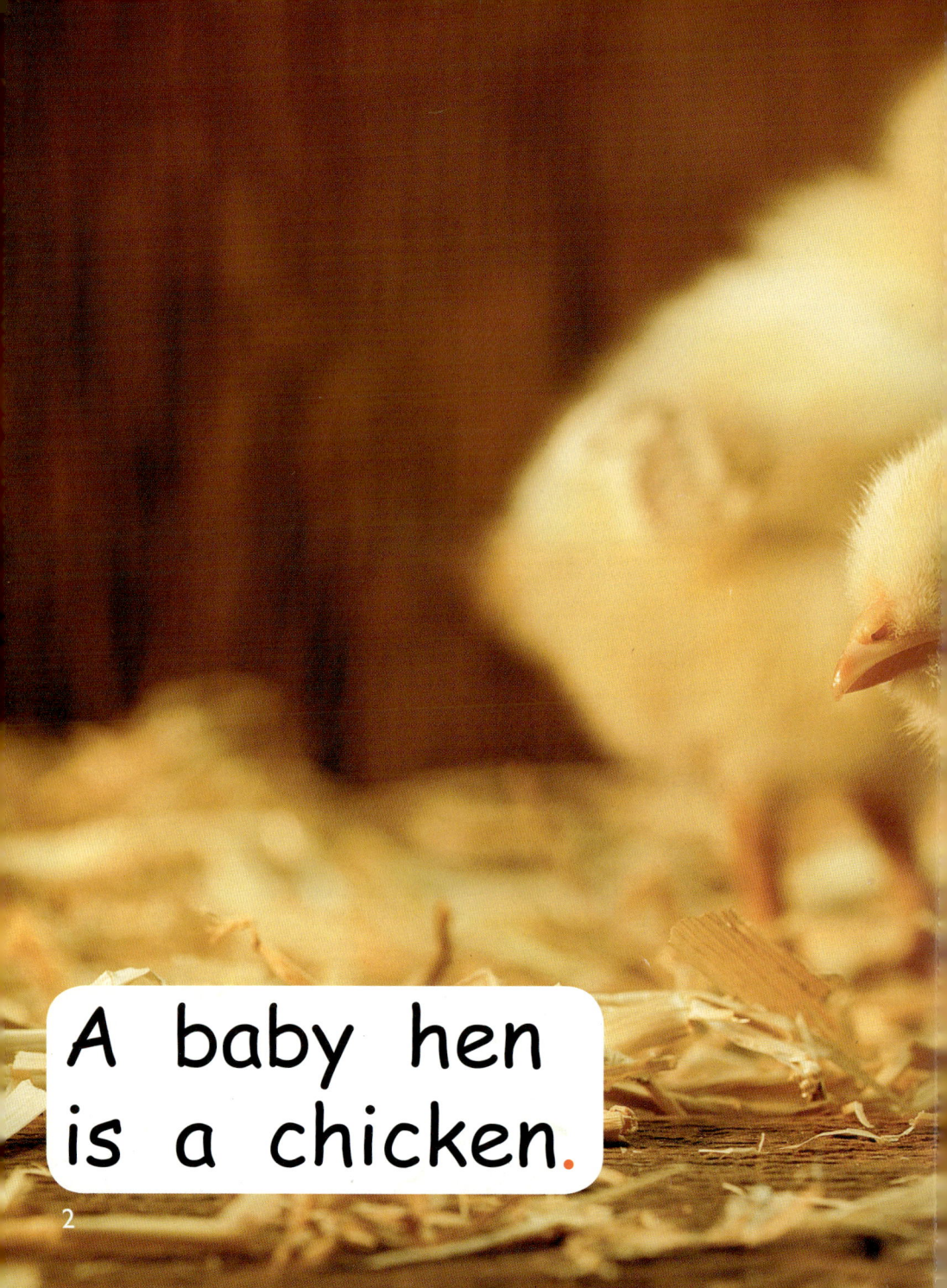

A baby hen is a chicken.

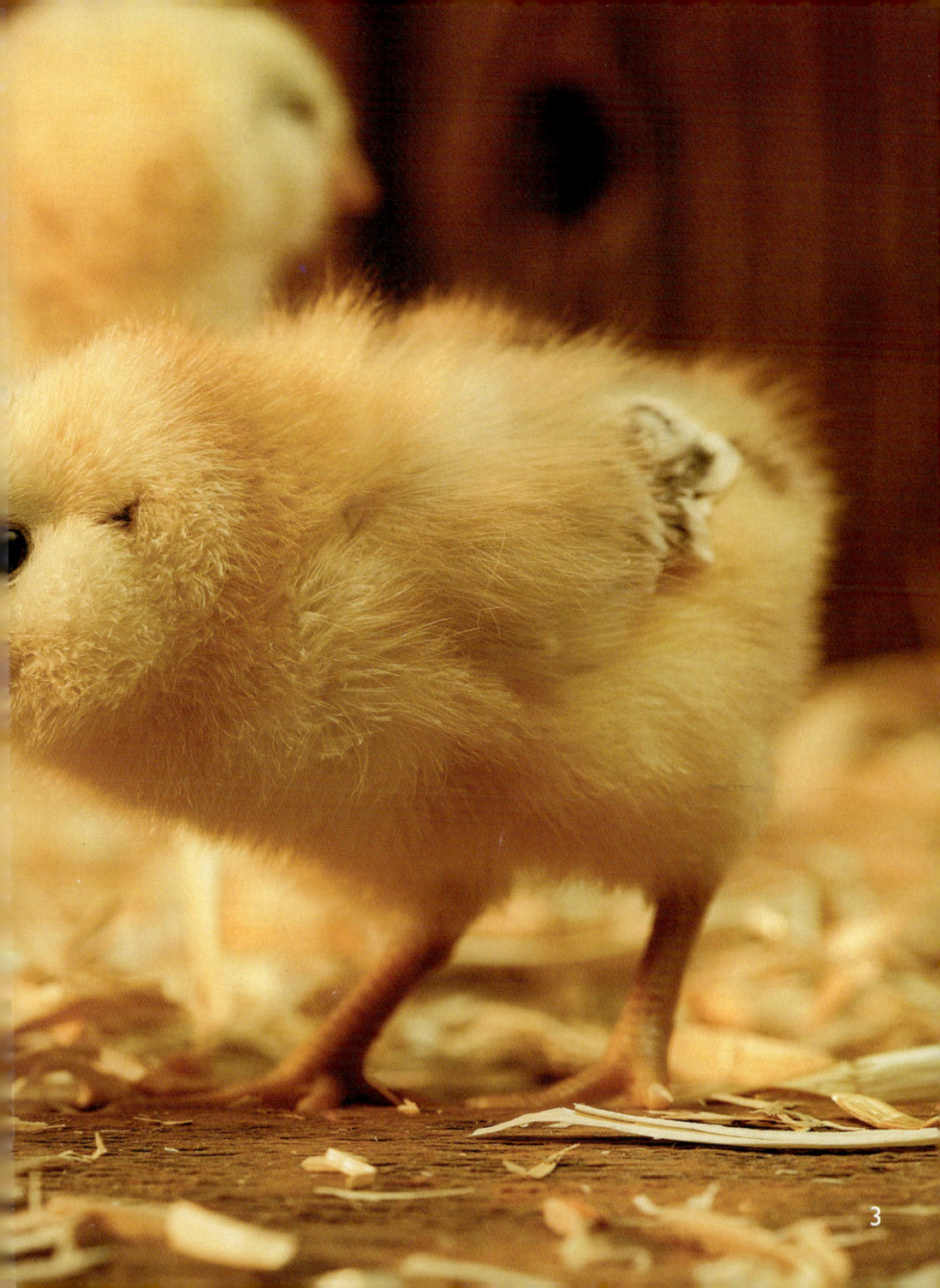

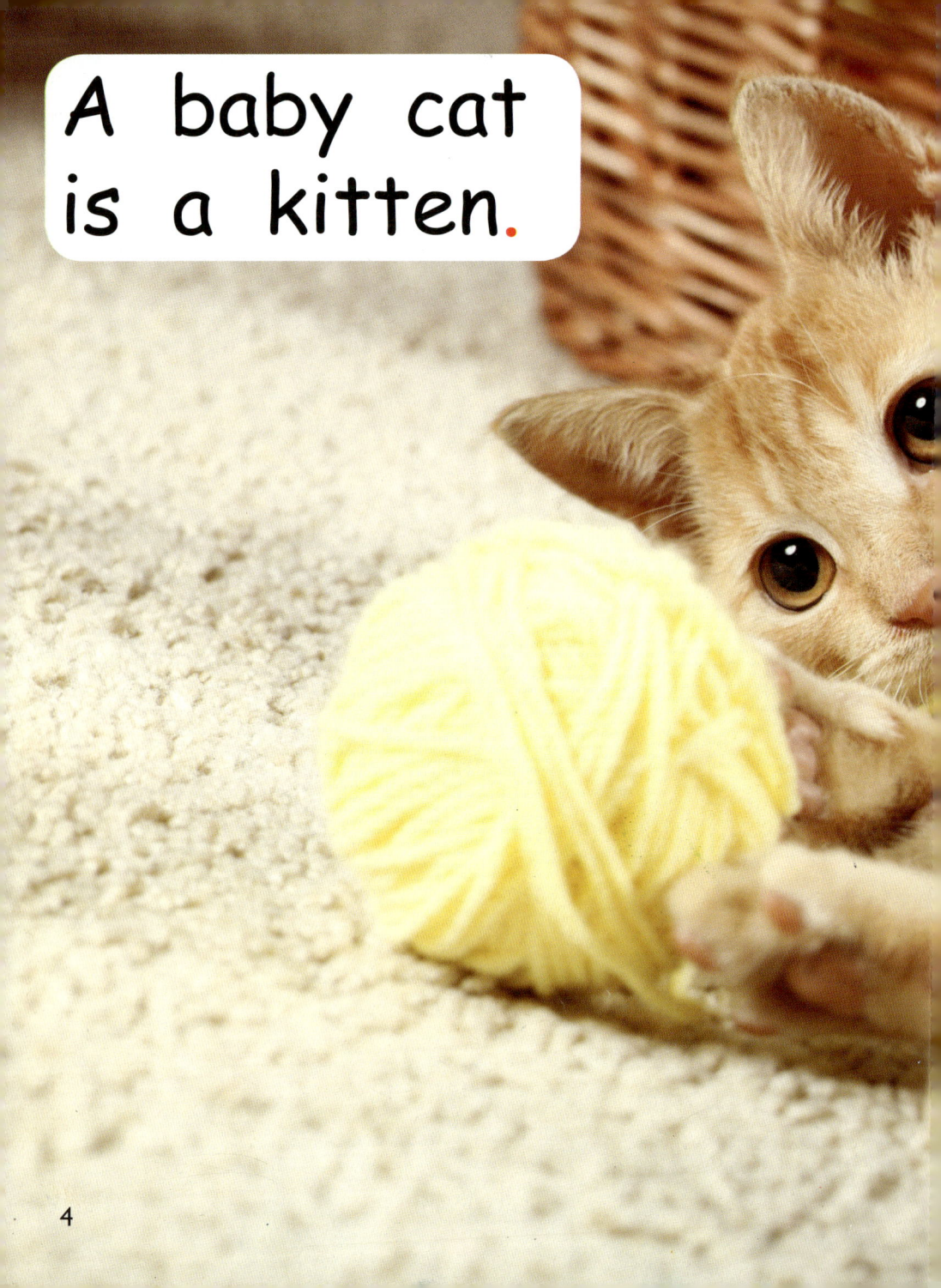

A baby cat is a kitten.

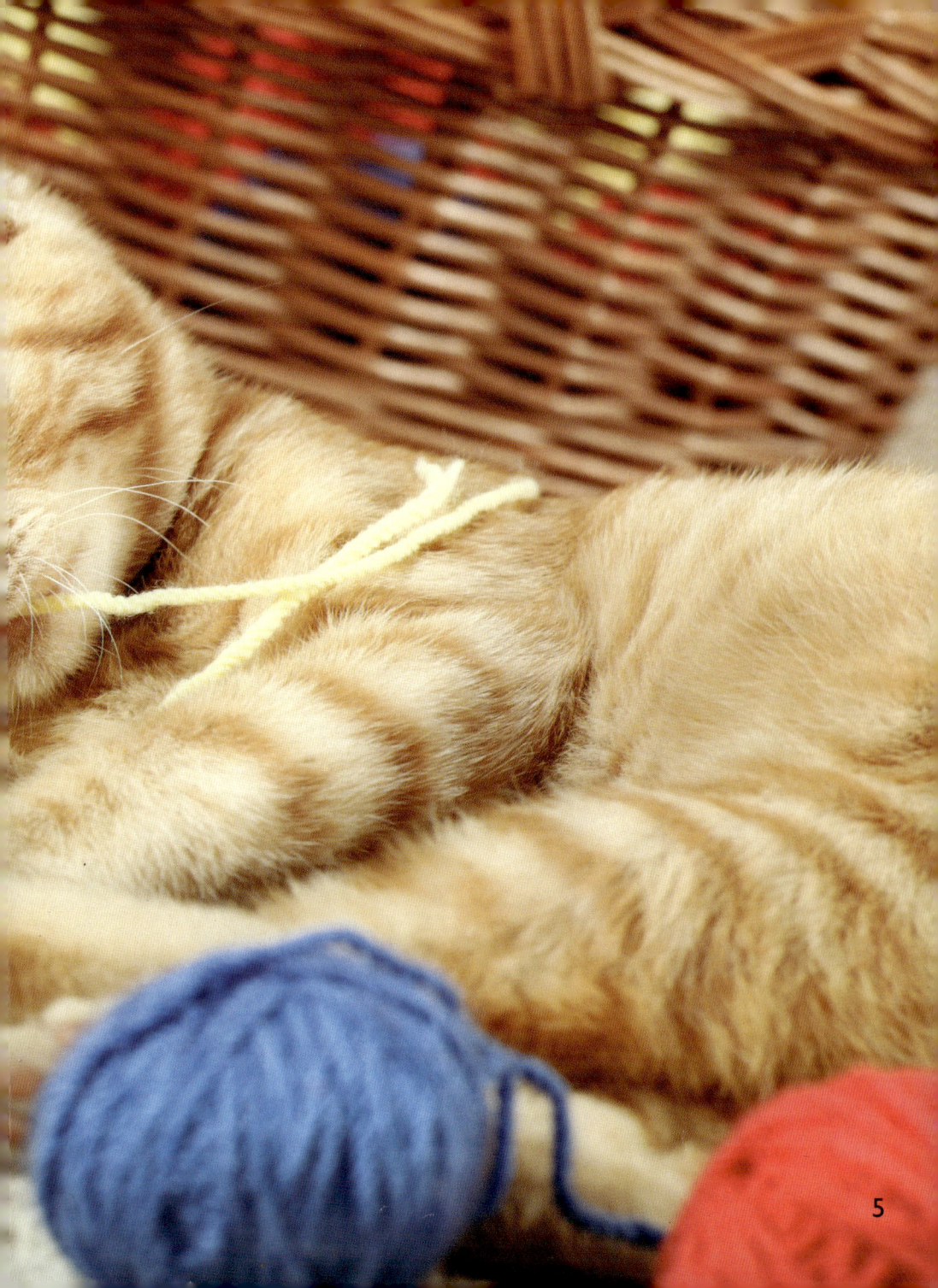

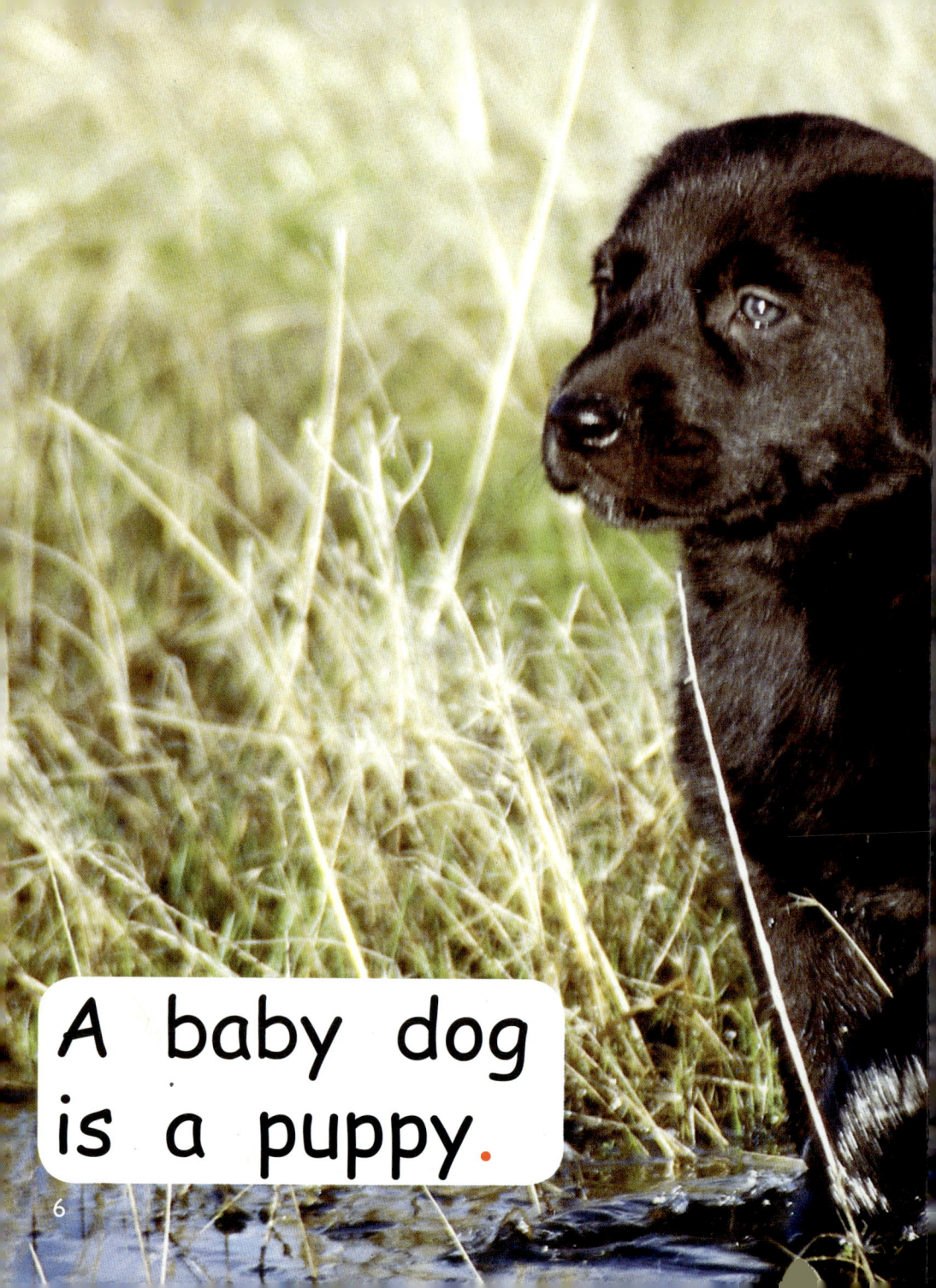

A baby dog is a puppy.

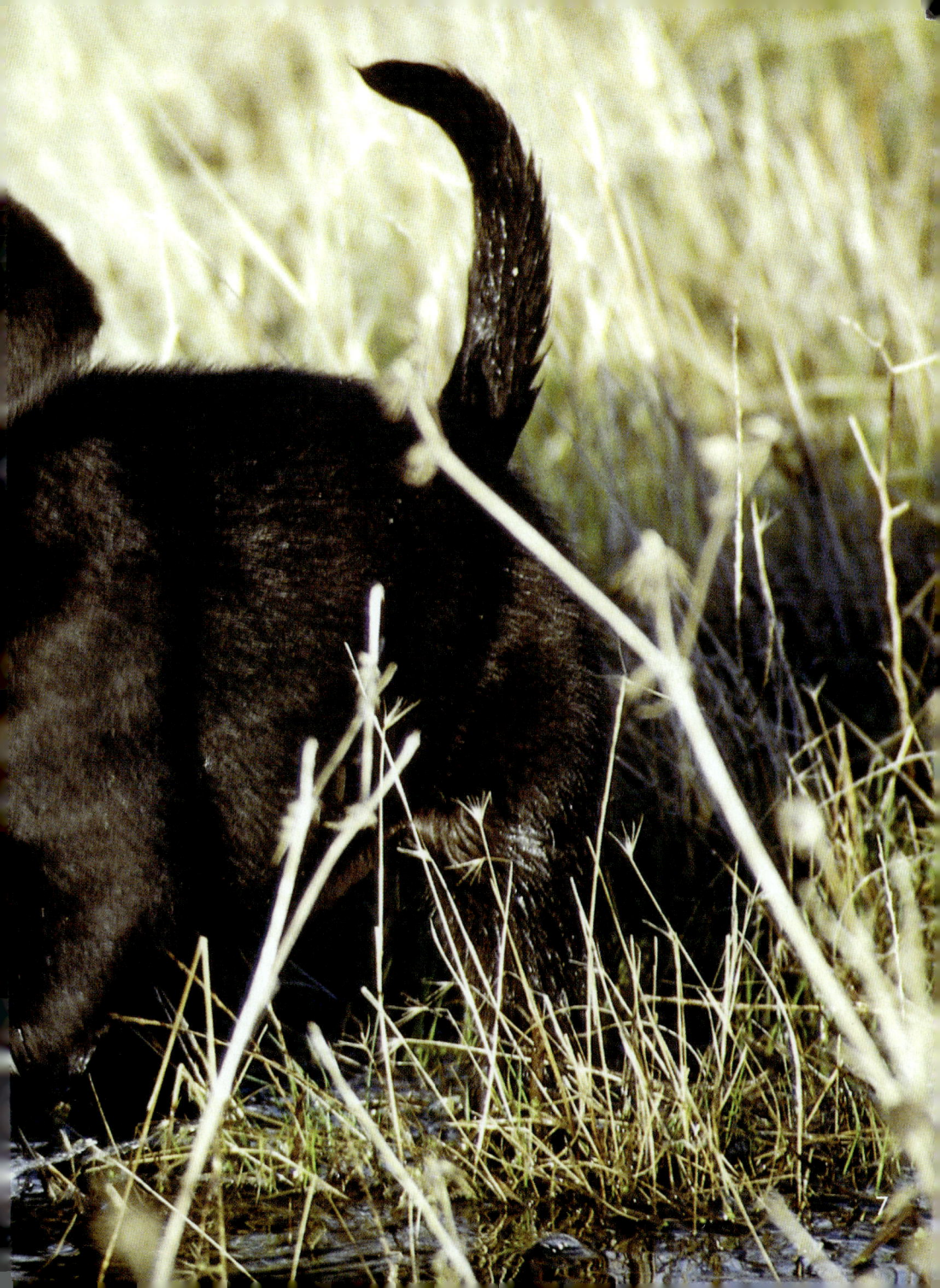

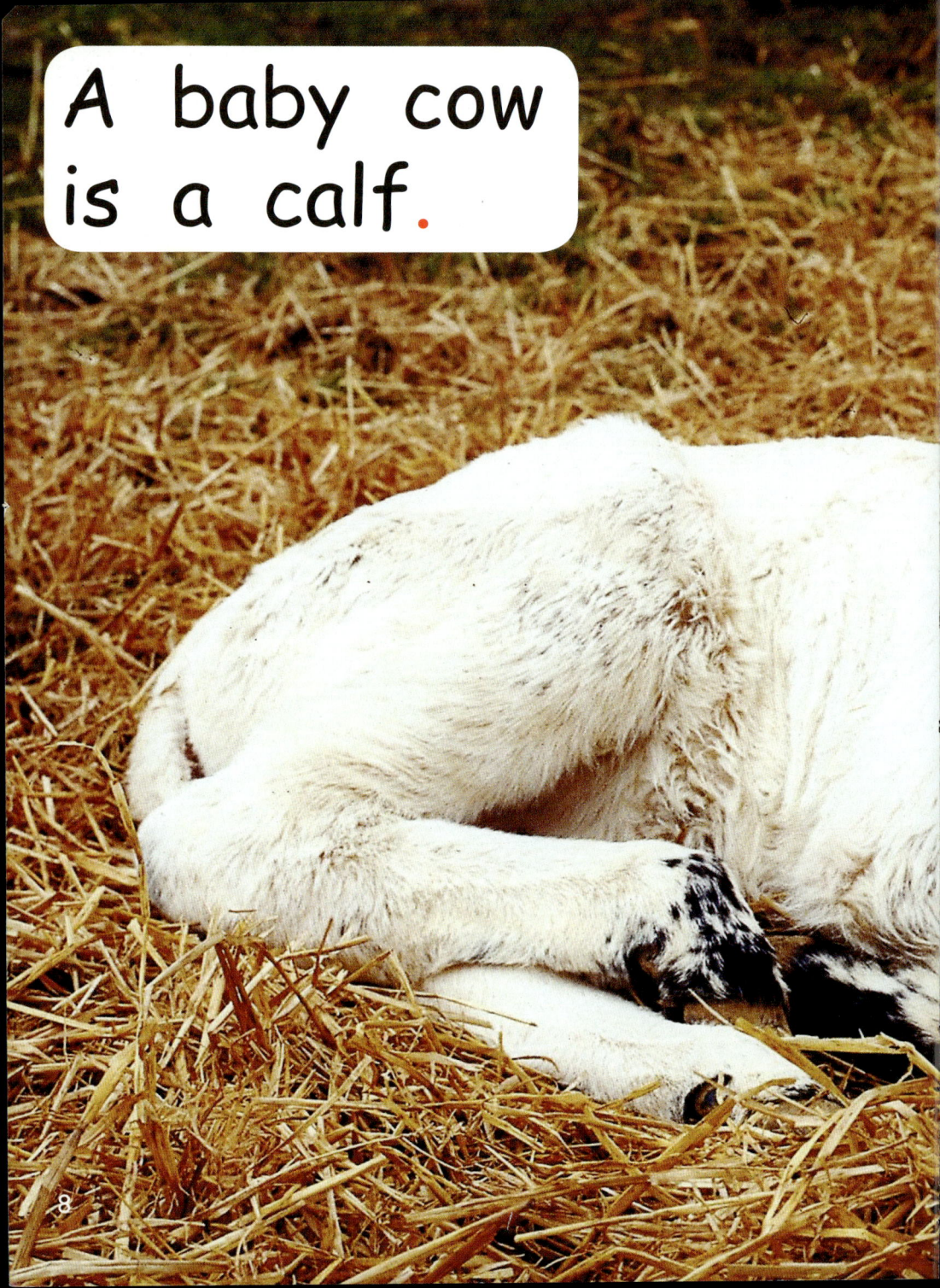

A baby cow is a calf.

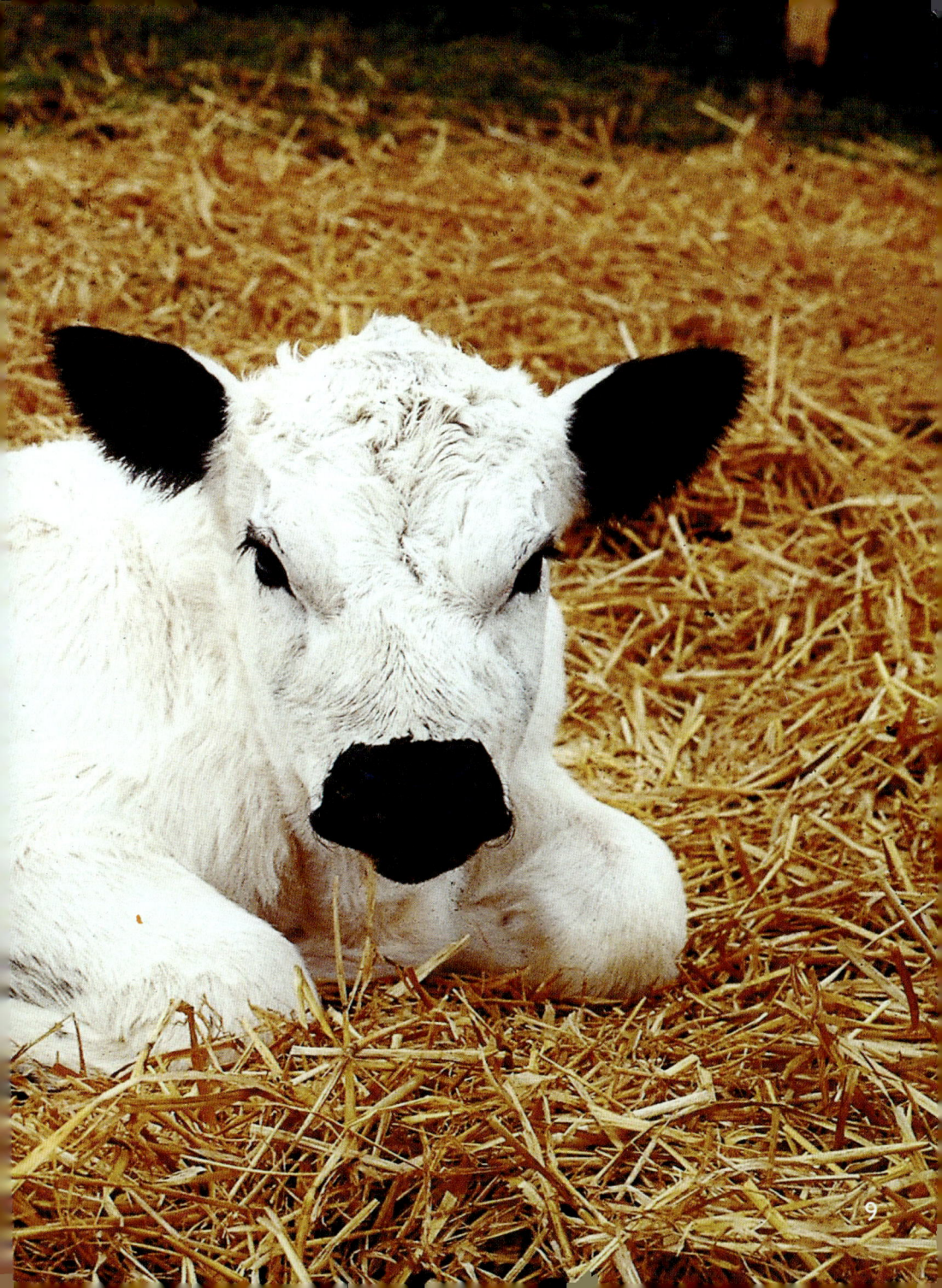

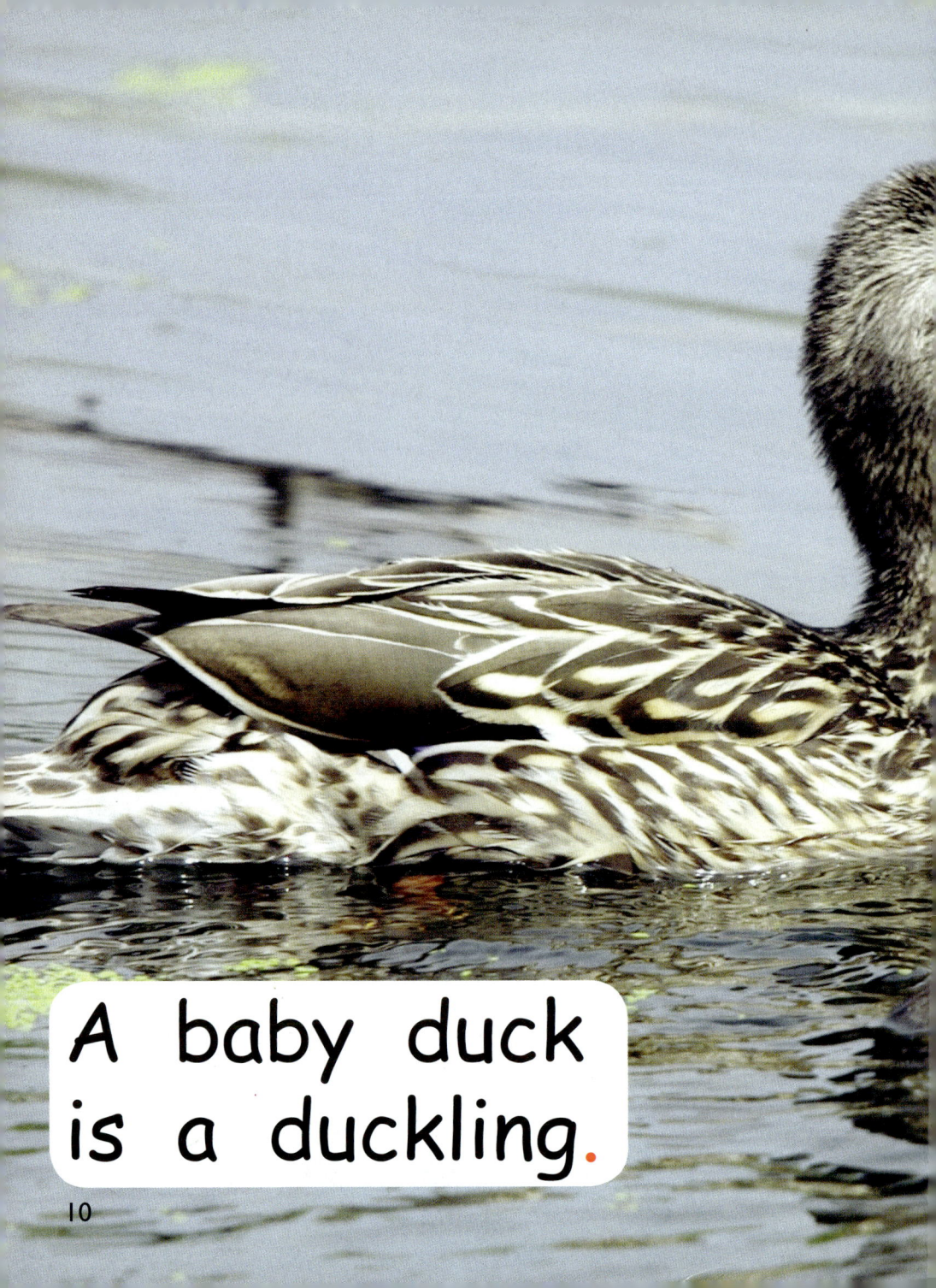

A baby duck
is a duckling.

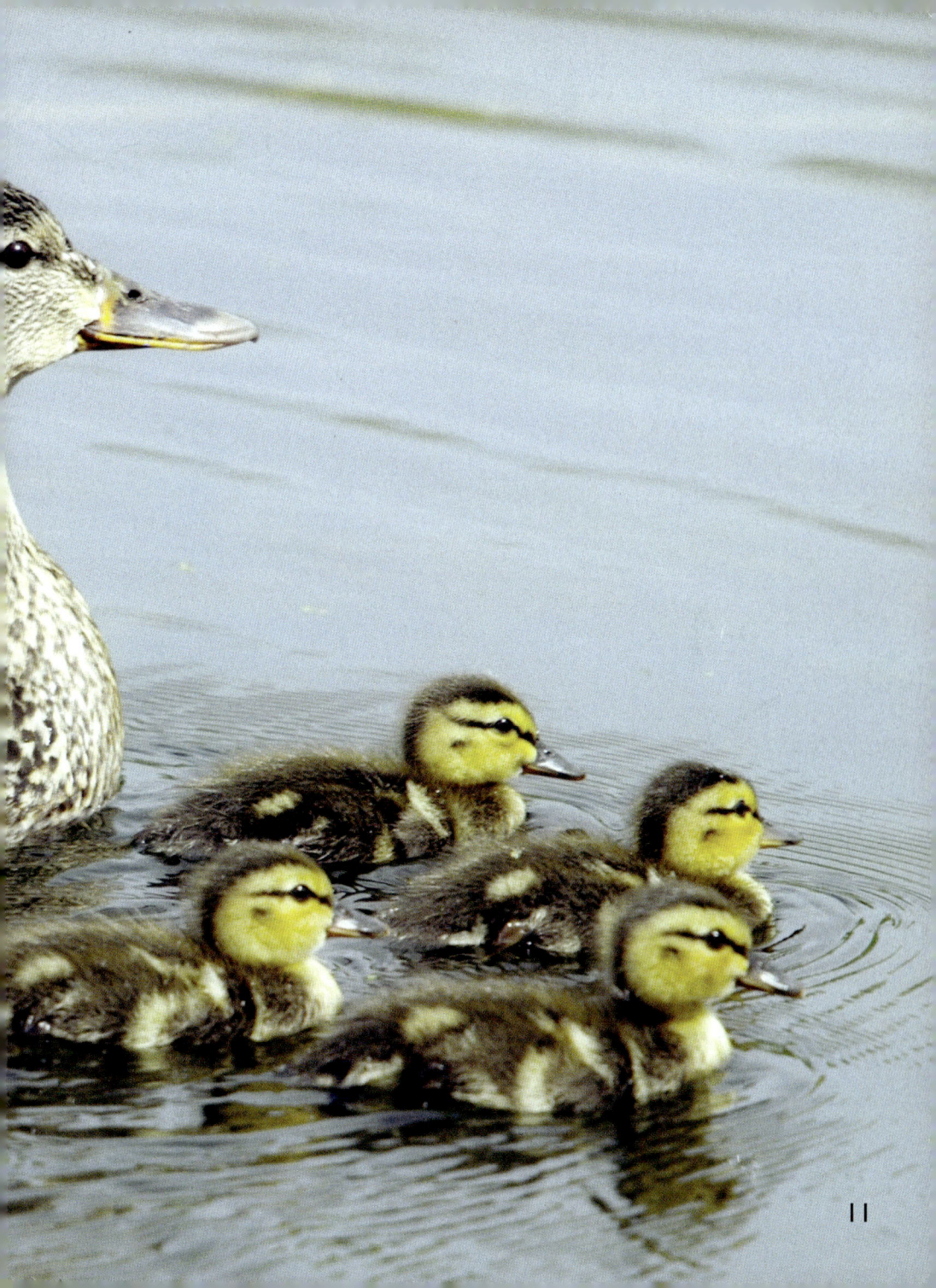

11

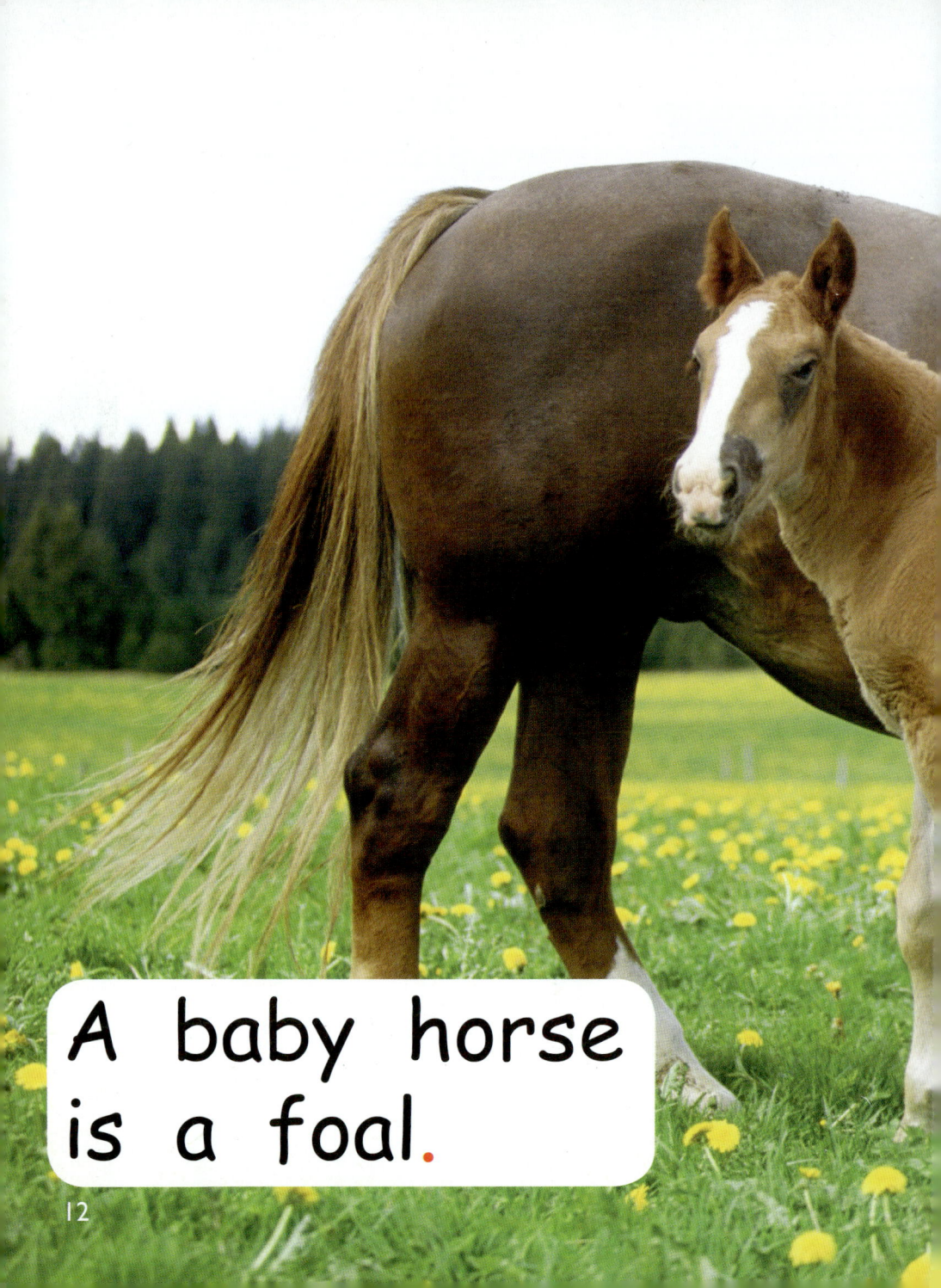

A baby horse is a foal.

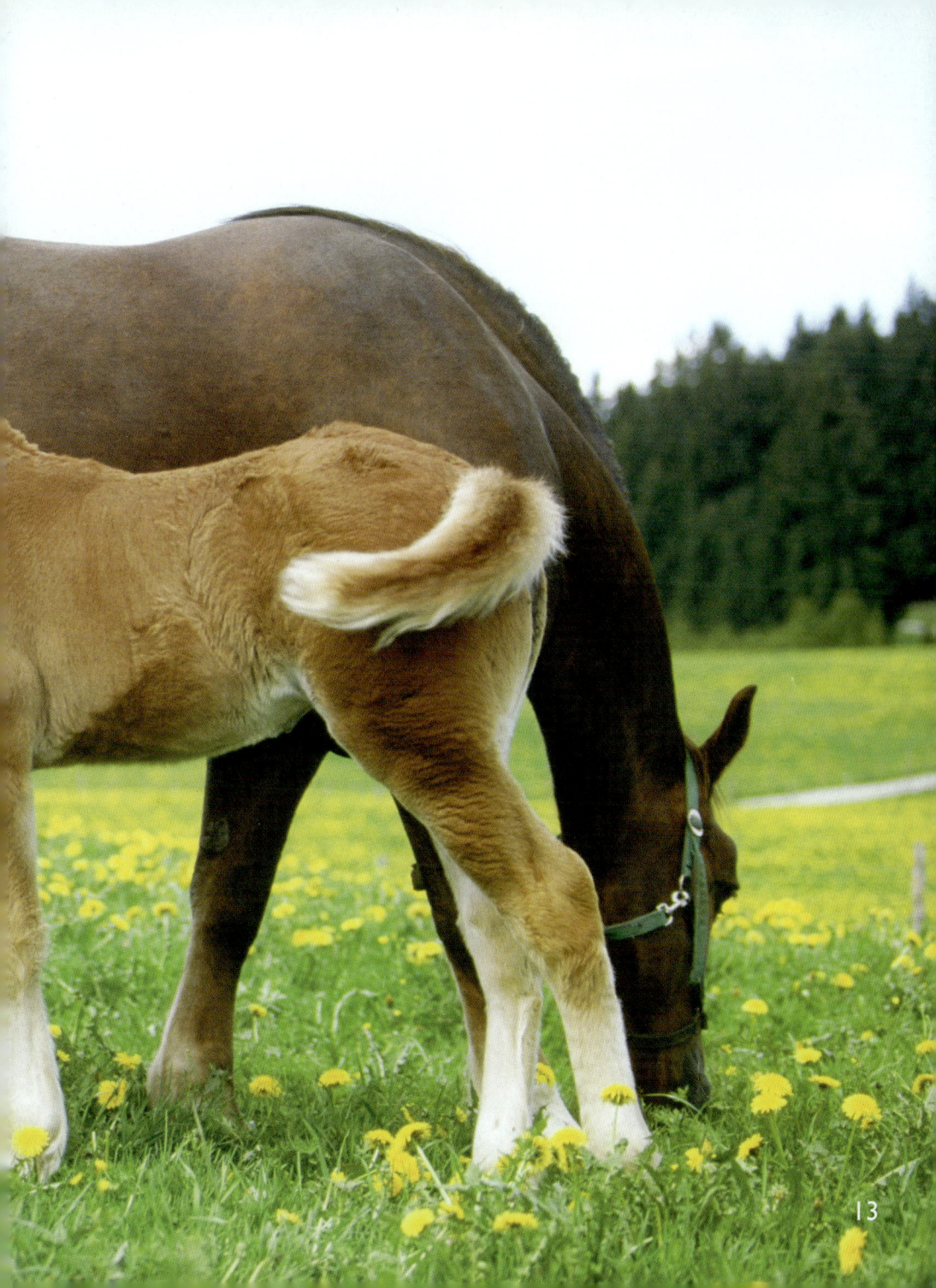

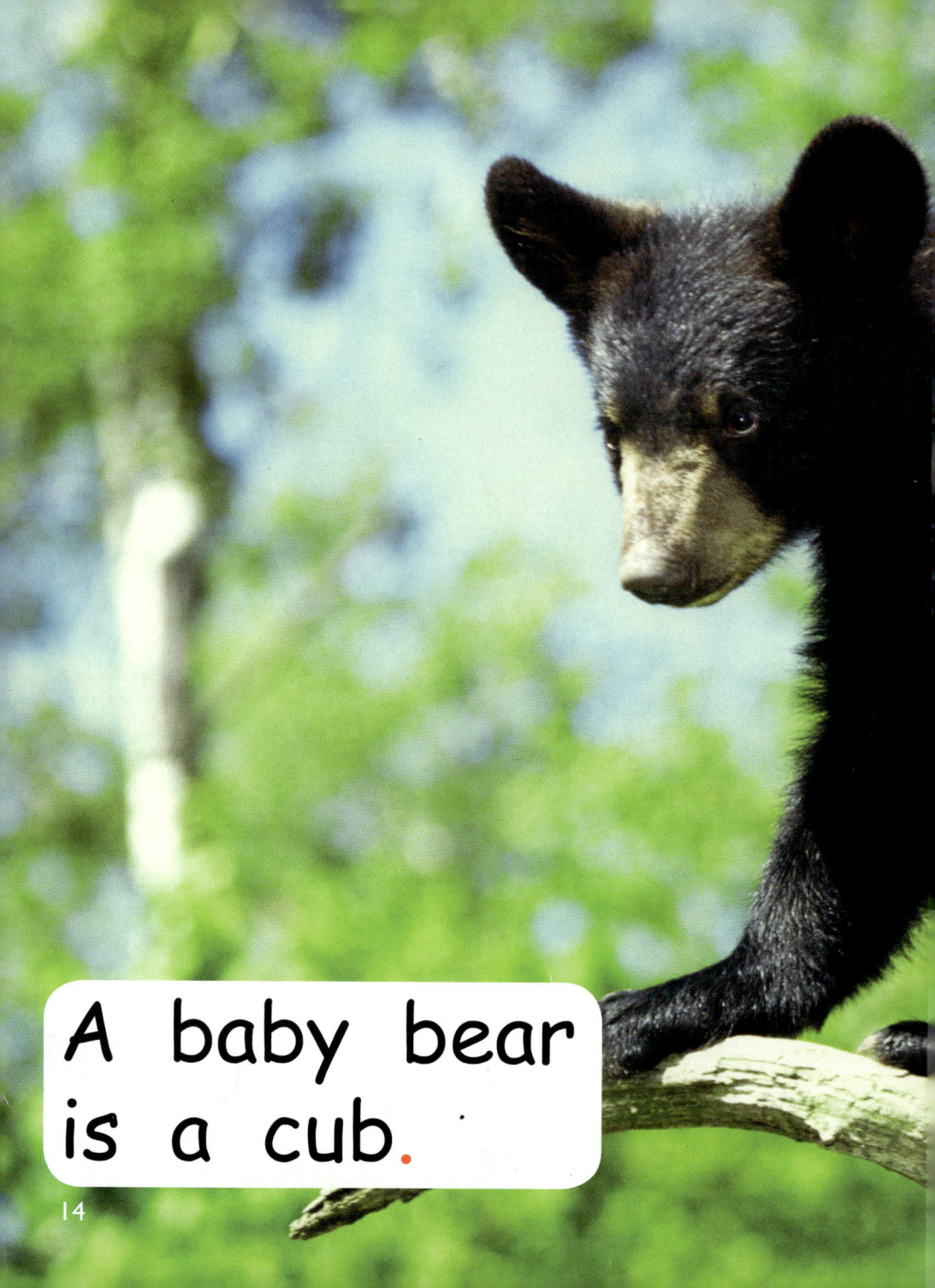

A baby bear is a cub.

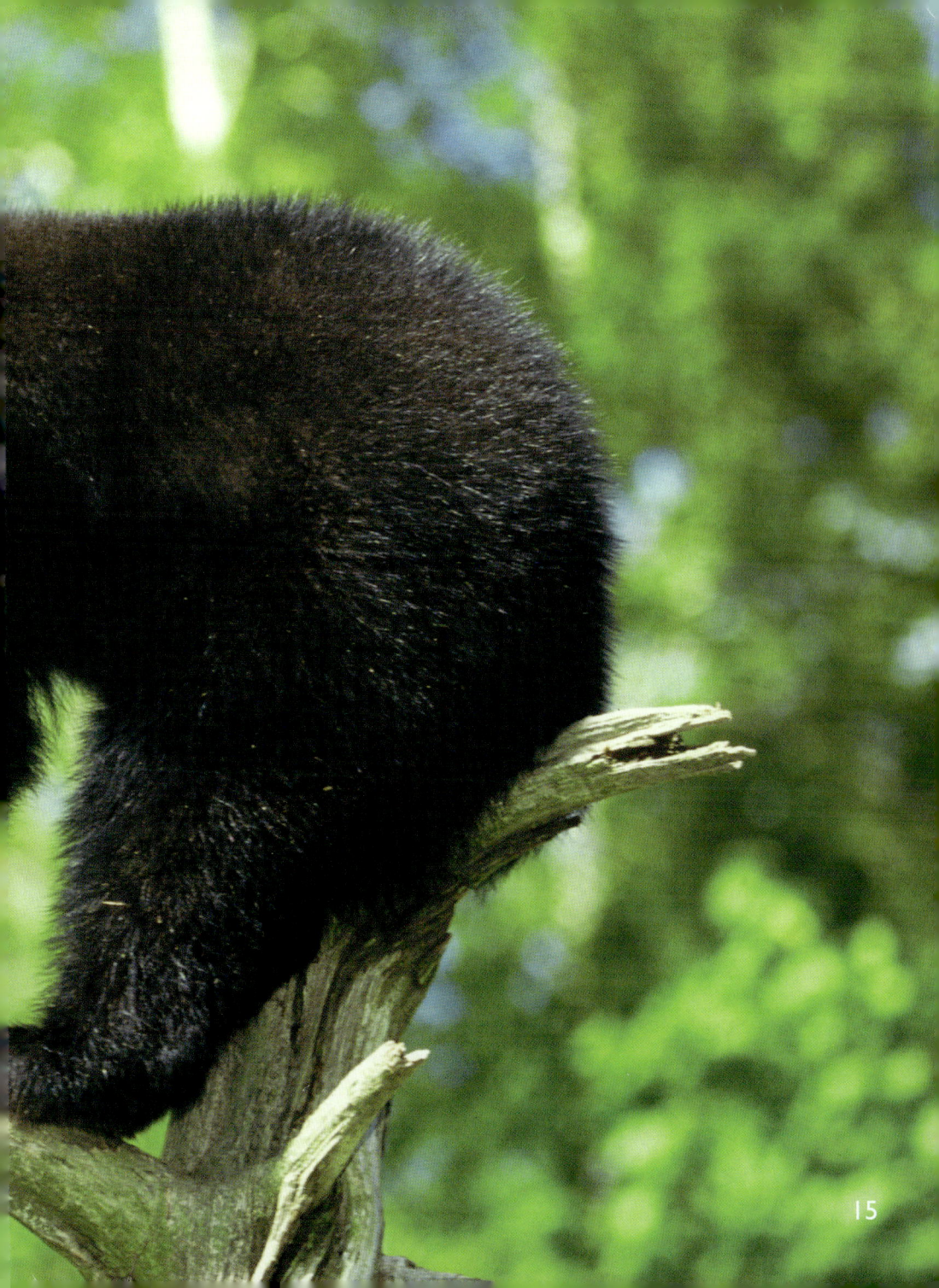

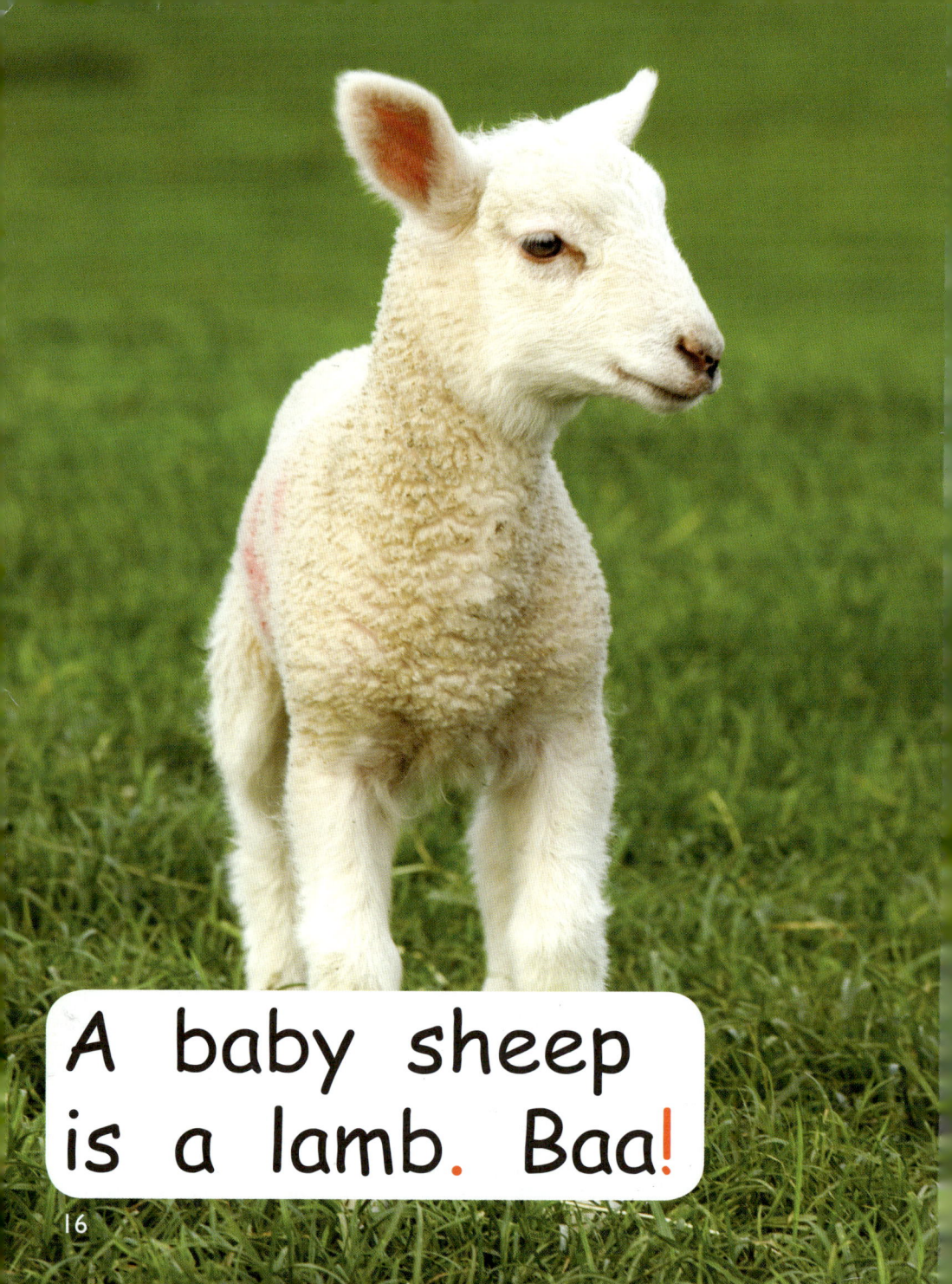

A baby sheep
is a lamb. Baa!